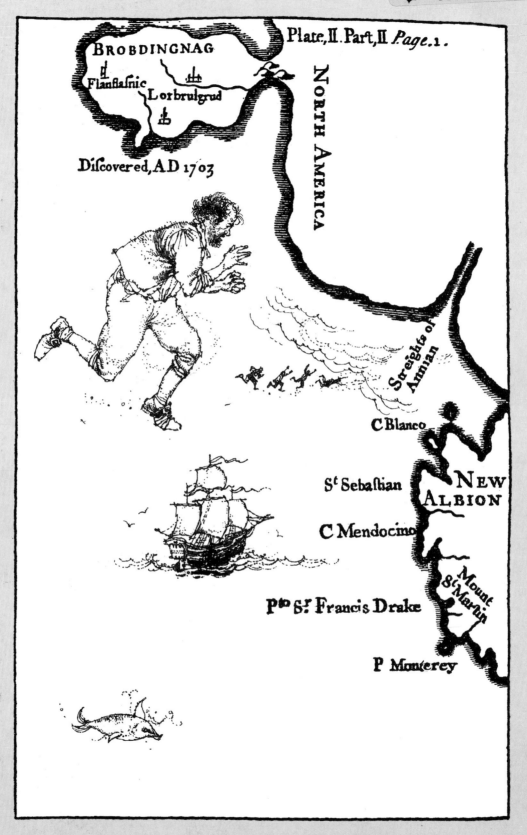

BROBDINGNAG

Flanflasnic

Lorbrulgrud

Discovered, A.D 1703

Plate, II. Part, II Page. 1.

NORTH AMERICA

Streights of Anmian

C. Blanco

St Sebastian

C. Mendocino

NEW ALBION

Pto St Francis Drake

Mount St Martin

P Monterey

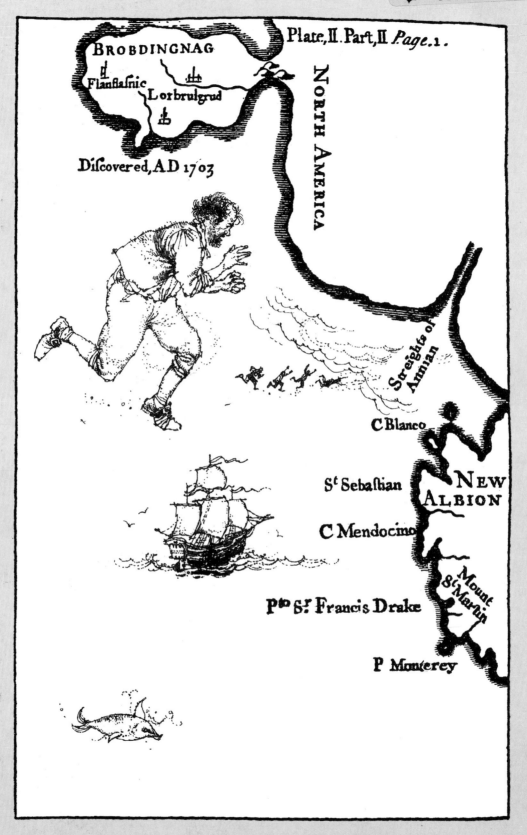

Gulliver's Travels

Jonathan Swift

Adapted by James Riordan
Illustrated by Victor G Ambrus

Oxford University Press
Oxford   New York   Toronto

Oxford University Press, Walton Street, Oxford OX2 6DP
Oxford New York Toronto
Delhi Bombay Calcutta Madras Karachi
Petaling Jaya Singapore Hong Kong Tokyo
Nairobi Dar es Salaam Cape Town
Melbourne Auckland

and associated companies in
Berlin Ibadan

Oxford is a trade mark of Oxford University Press

ISBN 0 19 279897 9

Text © James Riordan 1992
Illustrations © Victor Ambrus 1992

Set in 11½/15pt Meridien Roman

A CIP catalogue record for this book is available
from the British Library

Printed in Hong Kong

Journey to Lilliput

Tied down upon the shore

The story I am about to tell is true. My name is Lemuel Gulliver and I was born in Nottinghamshire.

On the 4th of May 1699 I set sail from Bristol bound for the South Seas. I was ship's doctor on board the *Antelope* captained by William Pritchard.

Just north-west of Van Diemen's Land a violent storm blew up at dead of night and drove us upon some rocks. In no time at all the ship split up; but not before I and six crew rowed clear in a lifeboat. Our escape was shortlived, however. For within half an hour a great wave overturned our boat and my companions vanished beneath the waves.

Only I remained alive.

I swam as wind and tide directed; more than once, out of tiredness, I let my legs drop, but could feel no bottom to the sea. When my strength was all but spent, I found myself in my depth. It was a mile or so before I made land and once there I sank down upon the shore and fell into a sound sleep.

When I awoke it was already daylight. Lying on my back it took me a moment to get my bearings. Yet as I went to rise I found I could not move: my arms and legs were tied firmly to the ground! My shoulder-length hair, likewise, was fastened so tightly I could not even turn my head. I could look only upwards and the hot sun was burning my eyes.

All of a sudden I felt something on my left leg, moving slowly towards my chin.

Looking down as best I could I noticed a human creature no more than six inches high, holding a bow and arrow. Then at least forty other little men started to run all over my body. I was so startled I let out a mighty yell which sent them scuttling back again. However, they soon returned; one of them came right up to my face and cried out in a shrill voice:

'Hekinah degul!'

The others repeated the same words several times, though I had no idea what they meant.

At length, struggling to break free, I managed to pull up the ropes that bound my hair and left arm to the ground. At this the tiny creatures ran off before I could seize any of them. Yet at a command – 'Tolgo fonac!' – a shower of arrows flew through the air and landed on my hands and face. It was like being pricked by a hundred sharp needles. As I again tried to break loose, an even thicker volley of arrows showered down on me, and little soldiers stuck my ribs with their spears.

I thought it wise to lie still.

The arrows ceased. Meanwhile, I could hear knocking and hammering going on just by my right ear; by turning my head slightly I could see a sort of wooden stage with three ladders leading up to it. When it was ready, a tiny fellow no taller than my middle finger mounted the stage and cried out three times:

'Langro dehul san.'

Then this 'Hurgo' – for so he was called – made a long speech of which I understood not one word. Finally I grew impatient. After all, I had not eaten for ages. Opening and closing my mouth, I tried to make the Hurgo understand my needs. At last he summoned a hundred or so men to bring baskets of meat to my mouth. No doubt they were whole carcasses of ox and sheep, yet to me they seemed no bigger than the wings of a lark.

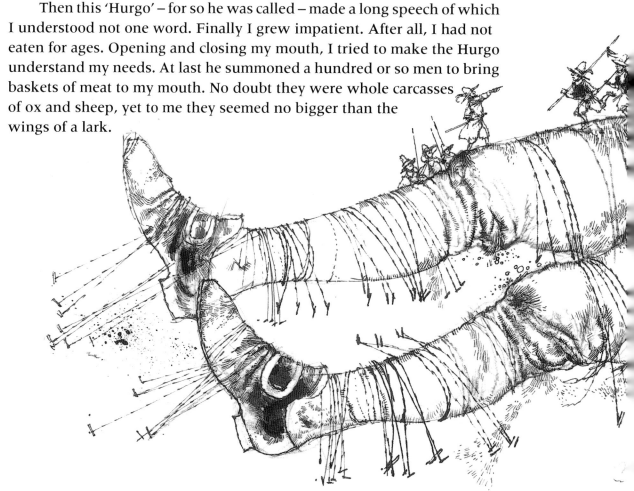

I ate them two or three at a time. And likewise the loaves they brought, which were no bigger than a musket ball. The little people supplied me as quickly as they could, marvelling at my huge appetite.

I then made a sign I wished to drink; and they rolled up barrels of wine: each was about half a pint and tasted really delicious.

When I had eaten and drunk, the little people danced with joy upon my chest, shouting out:

'Hekinah degul!'

Next they daubed my face and blistered hands with a pleasantly smelling ointment which soon removed the soreness of their arrows. By that time I was beginning to feel drowsy: no wonder, since, as I later learned, the wine had been drugged.

I fell into a deep sleep.

The moment I began to snore, some five hundred carpenters set to work to build a massive wooden trolley about seven feet long and four feet wide on twenty-two wheels. My sleeping form was raised on pulleys and ropes by nine hundred men on to the trolley and then drawn by a thousand of the King's largest horses (each about four and a half inches high). I was taken to a huge temple in the capital city; this was to be my home.

Thus when I awoke I found myself lying inside a great hall; there was no room to stand up. In any case my legs were hung with chains and thirty-six padlocks. I had just room enough to ease myself through the temple gates and stand up in the yard beyond. The chains enabled me only to walk round in a semi-circle.

By now, however, the most pressing needs of nature had me fit to burst. What was I to do? Imagine my shame at relieving myself in front of all those watching faces. . . And imagine their alarm at the torrents that poured through the temple yard. From that time on two stable grooms were appointed to remove the offensive matter in wheelbarrows each morning.

The King pays a visit

One day the King came to see me. He advanced on horseback, holding a sword rather like one of our darning needles; but the sight of me was too much for his steed, which reared up in fright. Yet the King bravely kept his seat until royal attendants held the bridle firm and helped him dismount.

The Queen, young princes, lords and ladies all sat at some distance watching the scene.

The King was taller by my nail-breadth than the rest, he had an olive skin, arched nose and graceful limbs. I would put him at some 28 years old. He wore a plain tunic and gold plumed helmet; his voice was shrill yet clear – not that I understood a word he said. I tried speaking in all the languages I knew, but to no avail.

It was clear that the King was deciding whether I should live or die.

After all, I would be very costly to feed and could eat them out of house and home; besides, I might be dangerous if I broke free. It would not be beyond them, I thought, to cut off my head while I slept.

After a couple of hours, the court retired and I was left with a heavy guard to watch over me. Some mischievous souls in the crowd about the square had the cheek to shoot arrows at me as I sat outside the temple; one just missed my left eye. The guards seized six of the culprits and handed them over to me to punish. Putting five into my coat pocket, I made as if to eat the sixth alive. The poor man squirmed and squealed for all he was worth, especially when I held my penknife to his throat.

But I soon put him out of his misery: using my knife to cut his bonds I set him and his companions safely upon the ground. I noticed that the soldiers and crowd were much surprised to see me treat them so leniently.

No doubt this action helped save my life.

I afterwards learned that the King and his Council had been debating my fate. At first they wished to put me to death; after all, they reasoned, I was costly to feed and might break free and cause havoc. So they thought of starving me to death or shooting me in the face with poisoned arrows. Then they reconsidered: my rotting body could result in such a stink as to risk a plague.

In the midst of their deliberations they received the news of my kind treatment of the six criminals. So I was saved. The King issued an order sparing my life and supplying my needs.

All the villagers for 900 yards around the city were to bring each morning six cows, forty sheep, bread and wine. My ration was fixed at exactly enough to support 1,728 citizens. Later I was told they had arrived at that figure by measuring my height and finding me twelve times bigger than them: thus, my body was thought to contain 1,728 of theirs.

They truly were an ingenious people.

Besides, the King ordered three hundred tailors to make me a new suit of clothes, six hundred citizens to serve on me, and six scholars to teach me their language.

Within three weeks I was speaking passably enough to talk to the little men, and I learned that the land was called Lilliput and the people Lilliputians.

The first thing I asked the King was to set me free.

He asked me to be patient; first I had to swear peace with him and his people. He also wished to have me searched – in case I was carrying dangerous weapons. Everything would be catalogued and returned to me in due course. Having no objection, I picked up the two search officers, putting them first into my coat pockets and then into every other pocket, save a secret pocket containing my glasses and some other personal items.

The officers wrote down everything with pen, ink and paper.

The Personal Effects of Quinbus Flestrin
(Man-Mountain)

1. A carpet large enough to cover the state room at the palace.
   (My handkerchief)
2. A huge silver chest full of sneezing dust.
   (My snuff box)
3. A great bundle of folded white substances the size of three men, tied with a thick rope and marked with black figures.
   (My notebook)
4. An engine and twenty long poles like palace railings.
   (My comb)

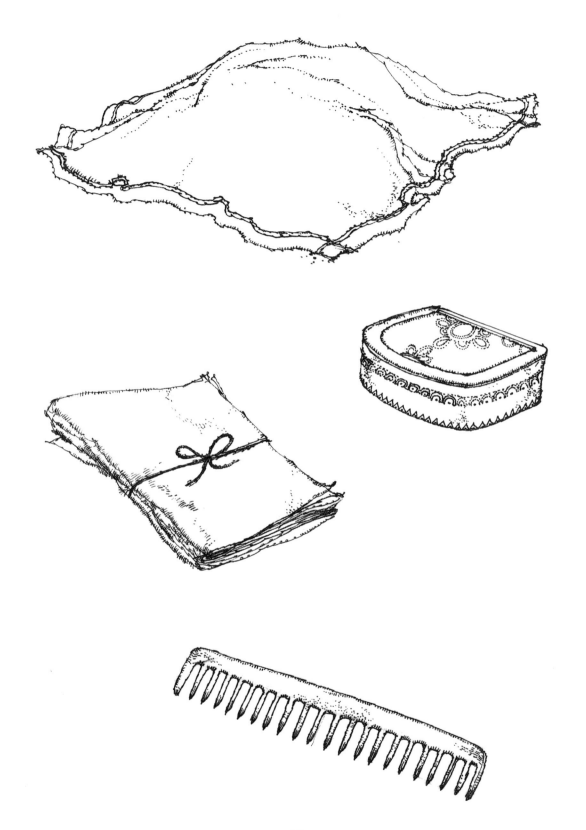

5. A hollow pillar of iron about the size of a man, fastened to a strong piece of timber and great pieces of iron. Two such.
   (My two pistols)
6. Two black pillars of irregular shape, at one end of which is an enormous steel plate. Both dangerous engines.
   (My two knives: one for shaving, one for cutting meat)
7. A great silver chain attached to a globe, silver on one side and some transparent metal on the other, bearing strange figures. This engine makes a constant noise like a water mill. It is either some unknown animal or the god which Man-Mountain worships, for he says he rarely does anything without consulting it.
   (My watch and chain)

8. A fisherman's net that opens and shuts, containing several massive pieces of yellow metal.
   (My purse and coins)
9. On his left side hangs a sword the length of five men.
10. On the right is a pouch with two pockets: one contains black grains, the other heavy metal globes.
    (My gunpowder and bullets)

Signed and sealed
on the 4th Day of the 89th Moon
of Your Majesty's Reign.

Clefren Frelock
Marsi Frelock

In no time at all the King himself arrived, asking me to draw my sword. I did so and at once all the royal troops let out a cry of terror. For the bright sun reflected on to my sword as I waved it above my head, so dazzling their eyes.

His Majesty, though, was less afraid, ordering me to place the sword upon the ground. Next he asked me to demonstrate the use of my 'hollow iron pillars'.

Warning him not to be scared, I fired one of my pistols into the air.

Hundreds fell down as if struck dead; even the King went as white as a sheet. He had me hand over the pistols instantly.

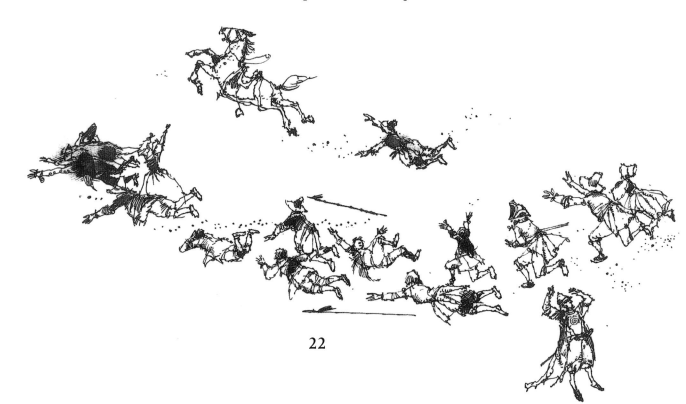

This I had to do with my other possessions; all except my glasses which I kept hidden.

Gradually the people came to realize I posed no threat. Sometimes I would lie down and let five or six of them dance on my hand, or boys and girls would come and play hide-and-seek in my hair.

They also put on a show for me: rope-walkers performed upon a slender white thread held about a foot from the ground. The interesting thing is that all the ministers at court are chosen for their balancing acts: the ones who show greatest skill at balancing and walking the tightrope gain the top jobs. Every so often they have to take tests to prove their skill and fitness; not infrequently they fall and break a limb or even break their neck.

On one occasion riders from the royal stables leapt over my hand as I held it on the ground; one even cleared my foot, shoe and all – a prodigious leap.

Two days later the King ordered his generals to march his army between my legs as I stood like a colossus: no fewer than three thousand foot soldiers two dozen abreast and a thousand horsemen sixteen abreast. For this spectacle I lifted up the King and, after much persuasion, even the Queen in her chair so as to give them a better view.

Big Enders and Small Enders

Not long after, the King agreed to set me free. I had to swear to obey certain rules, first in the manner of my own country, and then in their fashion. This latter was most peculiar.

I had to hold my right foot in my left hand, place the middle finger of my right hand on the top of my head, and my thumb on the tip of my right ear.

That done, my chains were unlocked and I was set free.

The first thing I did was to ask to see Mildendo, the capital city. Permission was granted and the citizens were told to stay indoors in case I trod on them; I stepped over the Western Gate and passed gingerly through the main streets. The garrets and tops of houses were so packed with people that I thought I had never seen a more crowded place in all my travels.

The city held some half a million souls, its houses were from three to five storeys high, its shops and markets full of stalls and provisions.

The King's palace was in the centre of the city, where the two main streets met, surrounded by a wall two feet high. Having reached the innermost court, I lay down on my side and looked in at the open windows. I saw the most splendid chambers that can be imagined. The Queen herself came to a window, smiled graciously and gave me her hand to kiss.

One morning soon after, I had a visit from Reldresal, one of the King's top ministers. We talked for an hour as I held him in my hand: he told me of two evils threatening the country – one at home and one abroad.

'As to the first,' he said, 'for some seventy moons past, there have been two struggling parties in our Empire: Tramecksan and Slamecksan. The first wear high heels, the second low. Our King gives work only to people with low heels, and the high heels people are angry. So the one does not talk to the other.

'As to the second, we are about to be invaded by the people of the nearby island of Blefuscu. Lilliput has been engaged in a war with Blefuscu for thirty-six moons. It all began as follows: one morning, when our King's grandfather was a boy, he went to eat an egg at breakfast and cut his finger on the shell. According to ancient custom we always used to cut off the larger end of the egg; but after the prince's accident, it was decreed that everyone must break their eggs at the smaller end. Those refusing to obey had to leave Lilliput for Blefuscu.

'People so resented the small-end ruling that there have been six revolutions, one king killed, one deposed, and some eleven thousand people executed rather than submit to breaking their eggs at the small end. Many learned books have been written on the subject, and just as many have been banned. And the Blefuscu kings accuse us of going against the old ways and causing a split. In my opinion everyone should break open an egg according to their conscience.

'In this bloody war we have lost thirty thousand soldiers and sailors and we have killed even more of the foe. But now our King wants you to help us fight off the new invasion.'

I asked Reldresal to inform the King that I would aid the Lilliputians in any way I could.

During the next few days I studied the island of Blefuscu from the hill coast, listening to reports from scouts. Through my pocket glass I spied some fifty men-o'-war at anchor in Blefuscu Bay. I then consulted sailors about the depth of the channel between the two islands; I discovered that

at high tide in the middle it was seventy *glumgluffs* deep – which is just over my head; the rest was fifty *glumgluffs* at most.

So I laid my plans. I had fifty hooks and fifty cables made. These I slung over my shoulder, took off my shoes and stockings, rolled up my trousers and waded into the sea off the north-east coast. As I approached the middle of the channel I had to swim some thirty yards before my feet touched bottom again. In half an hour I arrived at the enemy fleet.

The sailors were so scared out of their wits when they saw me that they all jumped overboard and swam ashore, where a good thirty thousand people were gathered. I then set about attaching a hook and line to each ship's prow. All the while I had to fend off thousands of tiny arrows. Many struck my hands and face, and could well have blinded me but for the glasses I had put on.

Once I had fixed all the hooks, I tied the ends of all fifty lines together and began to pull the ships after me. Nothing happened. Only then did I realize that the anchors held them fast; so I had to brave the arrow-pricks once more as I cut each anchor rope with my knife.

Taking up the knotted end of the fifty lines again, I started to wade back to Lilliput, towing the ships behind me. The Belfuscudians were initially astonished at the sight of their whole fleet floating away; then they screamed out in grief and despair, hopping up and down with rage. Once out of range of the archers, I halted to pick out the arrows sticking in my face and hands. And I dabbed on some of the ointment given me on my arrival at Lilliput. That done, I removed my glasses, swam the middle of the channel, and made the royal port of Lilliput safely.

In the meantime the King and his entire court were waiting on the shore. At first all they saw was the fleet of ships bearing down on them. Since only my head was above water they thought it was my dead body floating in the sea. But as the channel grew shallower, I gradually rose out of the water, pulling the ships behind me. When I was within hearing range, I cried out:

'Long live the King of Lilliput!'

The King was so delighted he made me a Nardac on the spot, which is the highest title in the kingdom, a sort of Duke. But not satisfied with this success, the King now ordered me to return and destroy all the enemy's defences. He said he would rule the world, make all Big Enders break their eggs at the small end, and kill all who refused.

Nothing is so boundless as the ambition of kings.

I protested that I would never take part in forcing a free and brave people into slavery. I did not think it right.

My refusal clearly upset the King. Although he abandoned his plans, he began to harbour a grudge that was to bode ill for me later. How easily kings forget past services when their will is thwarted.

About three weeks later, a peace party arrived from Blefuscu and a treaty was signed. No doubt the envoys had heard of my friendly act towards them in preventing an invasion, because they invited me to visit their kingdom and show them proof of my great strength.

I willingly agreed to make such a visit as soon as I was able.

This obviously displeased the King of Lilliput. I had no idea then of the grave danger I was putting myself in or of the terrible fate awaiting me.

Lilliput and its people

At this juncture I wish to say something about Lilliput and its inhabitants.

While the common size of Lilliputians is under six inches, all the animals, as well as the plants and trees, are accordingly small in proportion to the people. For instance, the tallest horses and cows are about four inches, the sheep an inch and a half, the geese about the size of a sparrow, and so on downwards until you come to the smallest which were almost invisible to me. Thus, I would see a girl threading an invisible needle with invisible thread.

I shall say little of their learning, which for many ages has flourished in all the sciences. But their manner of writing is worthy of mention. Lilliputians do not write from left to right, like Europeans; nor right to left, like Arabs; nor from up to down, like the Chinese. They write slantwise from one corner of the paper to the other, not unlike some English ladies I know.

They bury their dead with the heads pointing downwards, since they believe that in eleven thousand moons the dead are to rise again. During that time the earth, which they think is flat, will turn upside down. So the awakened dead will then be rightside up and ready to walk away.

There are some laws and customs in Lilliput that are very peculiar and directly contrary to those of my own dear country. The first relates to informers, those who tell tales on others. If an accused person can prove his innocence beyond all shadow of doubt, the accuser is immediately put to a shameful death; and the innocent party receives all the property of his accuser as recompense for the loss of his time, for the danger he underwent, for the hardship of his imprisonment, and for all the charges he has borne in making his defence.

They look upon fraud as a greater crime than theft, and therefore seldom fail to punish it with death. For they say that care and vigilance may preserve a person's goods from thieves; but honesty has no shield from cheating. If a person breaks his word or trust, or tricks someone out of a sum of money, that is regarded as a terrible crime.

I once told the King that, in my view, a man who had tricked another out of a large sum of money was merely gaining reward for his cunning and enterprise. The King thought it monstrous for me to offer as defence the greatest crime imaginable. And truly, I had little to say except to make the lame excuse that different nations had different customs.

32

Although we usually call reward and punishment the two hinges upon which all government turns, I have to say that only Lilliput puts them both into practice. Whoever can show that he has strictly observed the laws of his country for seventy-three moons can claim certain privileges, a sum of money, and the title of Snilpall, which is added to his name. Lilliputians thought it a great defect with us that our laws are enforced only by penalties, and not by reward.

In choosing people for all jobs, they have more regard to good morals than to great ability. They say it was never intended to make the management of public affairs a mystery, to be understood only by a few persons of genius or high breeding. They suppose truth, justice, decent living, and the like to be in every person's power; the practice of these virtues would qualify any person for serving his country. By no means were intelligent people always the most moral and fit for office; just the opposite, they often tended to be the most corrupt and silver-tongued in defending their corruption.

Their notions relating to the duties of parents and children differ greatly from ours. They will never allow that a child is under any obligation to his father and mother for bringing him into the world. They believe also that parents are the last to be trusted with the education of their own children. So in every town they have public nurseries where all parents have to send their infants of both sexes to be reared and educated when they reach the age of twenty moons. These schools are of several kinds, suited to different classes and sexes.

The nurseries for male children are provided with grave and learned professors. The clothes and food are plain and simple. They are brought up on the principles of honour, justice, courage, modesty, religion, and love of their country. Their parents are permitted to see them only twice a year; the visit is not to last above one hour; they are allowed to kiss the child at meeting and parting, but not to bring any presents or toys, sweets or suchlike.

In the female nurseries the young girls are educated much like the males. They are therefore as much ashamed of being cowards and fools as the men; and they despise all personal ornaments beyond decency and cleanliness.

Nor did I notice any difference in their education, only that the exercises of the females were not quite so robust as those of the males. When the girls are twelve years old, which is the marriageable age, their parents or guardians take them home.

The cottagers and labourers keep their children at home, their business being only to till the soil; therefore their education is of little importance to the public. But the old and sick among them are supported free by public hospitals: begging is unknown throughout the Empire.

Here it may interest the reader to learn something of my own manner of living during the nine months and thirteen days I lived in Lilliput.

Having a mechanical mind, I made for myself a table and chair out of the largest trees in the royal park. Two hundred seamstresses were employed to make me shirts and linen for my bed and table, all of the strongest and coarsest kind they could get. Even so they had to quilt it together in several folds. They took my measurements as I lay on the ground, one standing on my neck, and another at my mid-leg, with a strong cord extended, while a third measured the length of the cord with a ruler about an inch long. Then they measured my right thumb; no more. They reckon that twice round the thumb is once round the wrist, and so on to the neck and the waist.

I was delighted to find the new shirt fitted me exactly, and likewise with the other clothes.

I had three hundred cooks to prepare my food; they lived in little huts built about my house, each preparing two dishes apiece. I used to take up twenty waiters in my hand and place them on my table; a hundred more attended below on the ground, some with meat dishes, and some with barrels of wine and other drinks slung on their shoulders, all of which the waiters above drew up by ropes, just as we draw buckets up a well in Europe.

A dish of their meat was a good mouthful, and a barrel of wine a reasonable swallow. My servants were astonished to see me eat the great hunks of beef and mutton bones and all, just as at home I would eat the leg of a lark. Their geese and turkeys I would usually eat at a mouthful; of the smaller poultry I could take twenty or thirty at the end of my knife.

One day His Majesty wished to bring his family to dine with me. They came in due course, and I placed them upon chairs of state at my table, just opposite me, with their guards about them. Flimnap, the Lord High Treasurer, attended there likewise, with his white staff; and I noticed he often looked on me with a sour face.

I have reason to believe that this visit from his Majesty gave Flimnap a chance to do me ill in regard to his master. He had always been my secret enemy, although outwardly he made much of me, especially before the King. Behind my back, however, he constantly reminded His Majesty that I was costing a million and a half *sprugs* (their biggest gold coin) and that the King should be rid of me before I ruined the kingdom.

My journey to Blefuscu

Soon after dining with the King, I learned to my sadness that my single-handed conquest of the enemy fleet had set some officers against me, especially the Admiral of the Fleet, who was jealous of my acclaim. These gentlemen now joined forces with my old enemy Flimnap, calling me a traitor for wanting to visit Blefuscu.

A council was called at which my enemies insisted I should be put to death. Painful deaths were proposed, three plans being favourite.

First, they would set fire to my house at night and burn me alive as I slept.

Second, some twenty thousand men would shoot me in the face and hands with poisoned arrows, so condemning me to a lingering, painful death.

Third, my servants would pour a poisonous juice on my clothes; this would make me tear out my own flesh.

Fortunately for me, however, His Majesty wished to spare my life. But he could not spare me punishment. He decided I would merely have both my eyes put out. Thereby my strength would be preserved and I would be forced to see by the eyes of the ministers, as princes often do.

The decision angered some ministers, who demanded a stricter punishment. In the end, the King decided I would be blinded and, in addition, slowly starved to death. That way, I would grow weak and faint, decay and die within a few months. They reasoned that the stench of my dead body would be less since I would be so thin. The moment I died, some five or six thousand Lilliputians would cut up my flesh and take it away in cartloads for burial, leaving my skeleton as a monument to posterity.

All this I heard through a friendly minister who came secretly at night to warn me.

I decided the time had come for me to leave Lilliput as quickly as possible. Without waiting for permission to go to Blefuscu, I went one day to the far side of the island where the Lilliput fleet lay at anchor. There I seized a large man-o'-war, tied a rope to the prow and, lifting up the anchor, set it drifting ahead of me; then I took off my clothes and laid them in the ship to keep them dry.

Towing the ship behind me, I waded and swam across the channel to the royal port of Blefuscu, where a host of people greeted me. Quickly pulling on my clothes, I asked the good citizens to inform their King of my arrival. I was given two guides to direct me to the capital city; holding them in my hands I followed their instructions until we came to the gates of the capital.

And there to meet me was the Blefuscu King and his train.

They all alighted from their horses, the Queen and the ladies from their coaches. None of them seemed to be afraid or anxious at my coming. I lay on the ground to kiss His Majesty's hand.

I explained I had come as promised with the King of Lilliput's full permission; and I offered my services to Blefuscu. I did not mention the trouble I was in.

My plight was soon known, however, for three days after my arrival, Lilliputian ministers arrived to demand my immediate return, bound hand and foot; I was to be executed as a traitor.

It was while the Blefuscu King was making up his mind what to do with me that something happened to decide my fate. I was walking along the north-east coast when I spotted what looked like an overturned boat drifting just off shore. Quickly pulling off my shoes and stockings, I waded out some two or three hundred yards and began pushing the boat ashore. Fortunately the tide was coming in and so helped me in my efforts.

When I reached the boat I could just hold up my chin and feel the ground as I gave the boat a shove; and so on until the sea was no higher

42

than my armpits. Eventually, I got the boat on dry land, and with a great heave, turned it upside down. To my good fortune, it was little damaged. All the same, I would need help to make it seaworthy.

There was nothing for it but to tell the King of my find and of my strong desire to return home. I begged him to give me materials to fit out the boat. No doubt relieved at having me off his hands, he at once ordered workmen to make two sails, ropes, and cables.

Five hundred workmen were employed to make sails for the boat, according to my directions, by quilting thirteen-fold their strongest linen together. For making the ropes and cables I twisted ten, twenty, or thirty of the thickest and strongest of theirs. In the meantime, after much searching, I found a great stone upon the seashore; this would serve me as an anchor. I received the tallow of three hundred cows for greasing my vessel, and I had some of the largest trees cut down for oars and masts; in this I was much assisted by His Majesty's ships' carpenters who helped me smooth them down.

In about a month all was ready and I took my leave of the King. His Majesty presented me with fifty purses of two hundred gold coins in each,

together with his full-length picture, which I immediately put into one of my gloves to keep it safe. The ceremonies at my departure were quite touching, with the royal family all coming to see me off.

I lay down on my face to kiss the hands of the King, Queen, and all the young princes and princesses.

I stored the boat with the carcasses of a hundred cows and three hundred sheep, with plenty of bread and drink and as many dishes as four hundred cooks could provide. In addition I took with me six live cows and two bulls, with as many ewes and rams, intending to breed them back in England.

I would gladly have taken half a dozen of the little people, but the King would not permit it. Just to make sure, he had all my pockets searched in case I tried to carry off his subjects.

Finally, I set sail at six in the morning on the 24th day of September 1701. When I had gone about four leagues to the north with the wind behind me, I spotted a small island about half a league to the north-west. This was about six in the evening. I cast anchor on the leeward side of the island, took some refreshment and went to sleep. I slept well – I reckoned for about six hours – and woke up at daybreak.

I ate my breakfast before the sun was up and weighed anchor. The wind being favourable, I steered the same course as the day before. My plan was to reach one of the islands that lay to the north-east of Van Diemen's Land. But I discovered nothing all that day.

Upon the next day, however, about three o'clock in the afternoon, I spied a sail steering to the south-east. I hailed her but got no answer. I then made all the sail I could, gained on her and in half an hour she spotted me, discharging her gun.

It is not easy to express the joy I felt as I saw her English colours: it was an English merchantman returning from Japan. As I drew alongside, I put my cows and sheep into my coat pockets and climbed aboard with all my cargo of provisions.

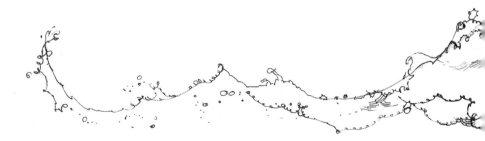

47

The Captain, Mr John Biddel of Deptford, was very civil and an excellent sailor. His crew comprised some fifty men; and as luck would have it I met an old comrade of mine, one Peter Williams who gave a good reference of me to the Captain. Although the Captain treated me with kindness, when I told him my story he was sure I was raving and that my time at sea had affected my head. It was only when I took the black cattle and sheep out of my pocket that I convinced him of the truth.

I then showed him the gold given me by the King of Blefuscu, together with His Majesty's full-length picture, and some of the other rare items of that country. I gave him two purses of two hundred *sprugs* each and promised, when we arrived in England, to make him a gift of a cow and a sheep.

We finally arrived in England on the 13th of April 1702. My only misfortune was that rats on board had carried off one of my sheep; I found her bones in a hole, picked clean from the flesh. The rest of my cattle were safe and I set them to graze on a bowling green at Greenwich, where the fineness of grass suited them well. Many people came to see the little animals and, after making considerable profit from showing them off, I sold them for six hundred pounds.

Since my last return, I find the breed considerably increased, especially the sheep, which I hope will prove much to the advantage of the English wool trade.

I stayed but two months with my wife and family. My insatiable desire to see foreign parts gave me no rest. So, leaving fifteen hundred pounds with my wife and fixing her in a good house at Redriff, I took my leave of her, my son Johnny and daughter Betty – with many tears.

I boarded the good ship *Adventure* – aptly named in view of what lay before me.

Journey to Brobdingnag

A storm drives me to the island of Brobdingnag

Our voyage on board the good ship *Adventure* went well until we reached the Cape of Good Hope, where we landed for fresh water. But, discovering a leak, we unshipped our cargo and wintered there. It was not until late March that we resumed our voyage, making for the Straits of Madagascar. But once through the Straits we ran into a violent storm which blew us off course.

We were utterly lost.

Although our food held out, it was not long before we began to run out of fresh water. So when one day the boy on the top mast spied land, we soon cast anchor and Captain John Nicholas sent a dozen men in the long boat to fetch water. I asked permission to go with them to explore the country.

When we landed we saw no sign of a river or spring, or of any humans either. While my companions went inland in search of water, I walked about a mile in the opposite direction over barren and rocky ground.

Seeing nothing of interest and feeling tired, I strolled back to the shore and was alarmed to see our sailors rowing for dear life back to the ship. I was on the point of hollering out to them when I caught my breath: a huge fellow was chasing them into the sea as fast as he could.

The water only came up to his knees; he was rapidly gaining on the helpless men when all of a sudden he must have stubbed his toe on some sharp rocks. For he let out a roar and stopped to rub his wounded foot.

In the meantime I ran back the way I had come as fast as my legs would carry me, clambering up the cliff. As I reached the top I was surprised to find myself amid grass as tall as a house. Thankfully I emerged on to what I took to be a high road, though it evidently served the local people as nothing more than a footpath through a field of barley. As to the trees encircling the field, they towered high into the clouds.

As I made my way across the field I came up against a thick hedge; it was while I was searching for a gap in the hedge that I heard someone advancing towards me from the next field. As he came into sight, I saw he was the same size as the one I had spotted in the sea.

He was as tall as a church steeple and took ten yards at every stride, as near as I could guess.

Not only was I awe-struck; I was trembling like a leaf. In an instant I ran to hide myself amongst the barley stalks, from where I had a good view of the giant. I heard him call out behind him; but the voice was so high in the air that at first I thought it was thunder. Whereupon seven monsters like himself came towards him with giant sickles in their hands – each sickle about the size of six of our scythes.

As the men bore down on me I quickly moved back, forcing my way through the tangle of yellow stalks until I could go no farther: wind and rain had brought down the corn, making it impossible for me to crawl through. And the beards of the fallen ears were so strong and sharp they pierced my clothes into my skin.

The reapers were not a hundred yards from me.

I was sure I would be squashed to death beneath a giant foot or sliced in two with a sharp blade.

I lay on the ground in terror, thinking of my grieving widow and fatherless children. How foolish of me to attempt a second voyage against the advice of all my friends and family. I could not but think of the Lilliputians who must have felt the same way when confronted by me.

How we fear as cruel and savage those bigger than ourselves! I was wondering whether I would end up as a tasty morsel in a giant's mouth. . .

Just as a reaper went to squash me flat, I let out a scream as loud as fear could allow. Thereupon the huge creature trod short and, looking all about him, at last noticed me as I lay trembling upon the ground. After considering for a while whether I might be a dangerous animal like a weasel that might scratch or bite him, he eventually picked me up by my middle between his forefinger and thumb, and held me a few inches from his eyes, so that he could see my shape more clearly.

55

I had the presence of mind not to squirm, even though he was pinching my sides painfully; for I was dangling in the air some sixty feet off the ground. All I ventured to do was to turn my eyes up to the sky, put my hands together in prayer and to speak in as humble a voice as possible.

As luck would have it he appeared satisfied, though curious at hearing me speak clear enough words, even if he could not understand them. All at once he put me gently into his top pocket and straightaway ran with me to his master, who was the farmer I had first seen in the next field.

The farmer took me from his labourer and put me softly on the ground upon all fours. But I stood up at once and walked backwards and forwards to let them know I had no intention of running away. They all sat down in a circle about me, the better to observe my antics. I pulled off my hat and bowed low to the farmer; I fell on my knees and lifted up my hands and eyes, speaking several words as loudly as I could; I took a purse with gold coins from my pocket and humbly presented it to the farmer, pouring six Spanish pieces and thirty smaller coins into his hand.

By this time the farmer was convinced I must be a human being. He spoke to me, but the sound of his voice was like the deafening rush of water in a water mill; I replied as loudly as I could in several languages. But we were wholly unintelligible to each other.

Finally, sending his men about their work, he took out his handkerchief, spread it over his hand flat upon the ground, palm upwards, signalling me to step into it. I did so, lying down full length upon the handkerchief, and in this manner the farmer carried me home.

At the farmer's house

Once the farmer came home, he called his family and pulled out the handkerchief with me wrapped in it. The moment he opened it, however, his poor wife screamed and ran away, just as English women do at the sight of a frog or spider.

Since it was dinner-time, all the family was sitting round the table: the farmer and his wife, their three children and an old grandmother. The farmer placed me in the centre of the table which was as high as houses from the floor. I was terrified of falling off.

The farmer's wife minced up a piece of meat and crumbled up some bread, which she put before me. I made her a low bow, took out my knife and fork, and fell to eat; that gave them all considerable delight. Then the mistress sent her maid for a thimble, which held about two gallons, and filled it with cider. I took up the thimble in both hands with much difficulty and drank to her ladyship's health, giving my toast loudly in English. Once more the company laughed heartily, almost deafening me in the process.

The farmer's youngest son, a mischievous lad to be sure, suddenly snatched me up by the legs and held me so high in the air that I trembled in every limb. Fortunately his father grabbed me from him and gave the lad such a blow on his left ear as would have felled a British troop of horsemen.

In the middle of the meal my mistress's favourite cat leapt into her lap.
I heard a noise behind me like that of a dozen whirring spinning wheels at
work; and turning my head I saw it was the purring of this cat, who
seemed to me to be three times larger than an ox. Luckily for me the cat took
no notice of me at all and clearly did not mistake me for a mouse.

When dinner was almost done, the nurse came in with a child of a year old in her arms; no sooner did it set eyes on me than it let out a squall that could be heard from London Bridge all the way to Chelsea. It wanted me for a plaything. To please the child, its mother picked me up and let the child see me closer; but it quickly seized me and put my head in its mouth. I roared so loudly that the urchin took fright and dropped me.

I would certainly have broken my neck had not the mother caught me in her apron.

As I looked into the faces of the giants around the table, it made me realize how ugly people are, with spots, pimples, and freckles that normally the eye does not see. It reminded me of the fair skins of our English ladies who appear so beautiful to us only because they are our own size; if we should examine them under a magnifying glass we should find that even the smoothest and whitest of skins looks rough and coarse and spotty.

That was how I must have appeared to the Lilliputians.

When dinner was done, my master went back to work, leaving me in the charge of his wife. She, kind soul, could see I was tired and put me on her own bed, covering me with a clean white handkerchief. I slept about two hours, dreaming I was at home with my wife and children. Suddenly I was awoken by something tickling my face.

It was a rat!

While I was sleeping, two rats had crept out from behind the curtains and run sniffing to and fro upon the bed. One of them was now touching my face with its whiskery nose. In an instant I was awake, on my feet and drawing my sword to defend myself. These horrible creatures now attacked me from both sides, and one clung to my collar with his forefeet.

But I managed to rip out his belly before he could do me any mischief.

As he fell down at my feet, his comrade made his escape, though not without receiving a good cut of my sword upon his back as he fled. These rats were the size of a large bulldog, but much more nimble and fierce.

Soon after, my mistress came into the room and, seeing me all bloody, ran to take me up in her hand. I pointed to the dead rat, making signs to show I was not hurt; at once she called the maid to remove the rat with a pair of tongs and throw it out of the window.

My mistress had a daughter of nine years old, and this little girl made a baby's cradle for me to sleep in; the cradle was put into a small drawer for fear of the rats. And this remained my bed for all the time I stayed with these people. The daughter was also my schoolmistress, teaching me the language. Whenever I pointed to anything she would tell me its name in her tongue, so that in a few days I was able to call for whatever I wanted.

Although the little girl was small for her age, she was seven times taller than me and as big as the tallest ship's mast. She gave me the name of Grildrig, which meant mannikin or little man. In turn I called her my Glumdalclitch, or little nurse.

It is to her I chiefly owe my survival in that country, and we never parted in all the time I was there.

It soon became known in the neighbourhood that my master had found a strange animal in the fields, about the size of a spinning top, yet shaped in every part like a human being, which it likewise imitated in all its actions. It seemed to speak in a quaint language all its own, had already learned several words of theirs, walked erect upon two legs, was tame and gentle, would come when called and do whatever it was bid.

One of my master's neighbours suggested he take me to town to show me off for gain. So he carried me to town in a box next market day, taking along his little daughter to look after me. The farmer stopped at an inn and, after a few words with the inn-keeper, hired the Grultrud (town-crier) to go through the town announcing the strange creature to be seen at the Green Eagle Inn.

I was put upon a table in the largest room of the inn, and thirty people at a time were admitted to watch the performance. I did as instructed: waved my sword about, turned somersaults, stood on my head, gave some speeches I had learned, drank the health of the guests, and generally made a fool of myself to please the people who had paid to see me.

I was forced to go through the whole rigmarole time and again until I was half dead with tiredness and vexation. The farmer made a great deal of money from showing me off every market day and then decided to take me on a countrywide tour. For some time I had but little rest every day of the week, save Wednesday which is their Sabbath.

About two months after my arrival in the country, which I learned was called Brobdingnag, I was taken to the capital where the royal family lived. And it was there that my fortunes took a turn for the better.

64

Life at the palace

It was not long before my fame reached the ears of the Queen. So one day a gentleman usher, or Slardral, came from Court, commanding my master to bring me at once to entertain the Queen and her ladies.

Her Majesty was delighted with my good sense, my polite conduct and handsome form. She asked me about my own country and travels, which I answered as distinctly as I could. Finally she asked whether I would like to live at Court. At that I bowed low and humbly put my lips to the tip of her finger.

Thereupon she asked my master whether he was willing to sell me at a good price. My master, being ready enough to part with me, demanded a thousand pieces of gold, which were given to him on the spot. But I begged the Queen to let Glumdalclitch continue to be my nurse and teacher. Her Majesty agreed and easily received the farmer's consent; he was glad enough to have his daughter at Court. The little girl could hardly contain her joy.

The Queen was so delighted with me that she took me in her hand and carried me to the King. His Majesty at once sent for three wise scholars to examine me closely to decide exactly what sort of creature I was. None of them could agree after studying me through a magnifying glass. At this point I asked leave to tell them and the King about my own country, where millions like me lived, where the animals, trees, and houses were all in proportion to the people.

At first the King did not believe me, but I convinced him in the end and he decided I was something special that needed looking after properly. After dismissing the three wise men, he ordered that Glumdalclitch should continue to look after me, since we obviously had a great affection for each other; she was given her own bedchamber at Court, a governess to take care of her education and a maid to dress her. But the care of me lay wholly in her hands.

Under my nurse's direction a sort of doll's house was made for me by the royal cabinetmaker: in three weeks he completed it, with several rooms, sash windows, a grand doorway, cupboards, elegant chairs and tables. The ceiling could be lifted up and down on two hinges. All the rooms were quilted on all sides, as well as floors and ceilings so as to prevent harm coming to me when being carried on journeys. I even had a lock on my door to stop rats and mice entering.

The Queen became so fond of my company that she would not dine without me. I had a table placed upon that on which Her Majesty ate, just at her left elbow; and a chair to sit on. I had an entire set of silver dishes and plates, knives and forks. During the meals my good nurse would attend to me, standing on a stool near the table. No other person dined with the Queen save the two princesses royal, one sixteen, the other thirteen years and one month.

Although the Queen complained she had a weak stomach, she would take up at one mouthful as much as a dozen of our farmers could eat in an entire meal; she would crunch a lark's wing, bones and all, even though it were nine times as large as our full-grown turkey. And she would put bread in her mouth as big as two twelve-penny loaves. She drank out of a golden cup that was twice my size.

Nothing angered and frightened me so much as the Queen's dwarf. Before I came upon the scene he had been the lowest creature in the realm; now he would swagger and look big as he passed me by, and make sneering remarks about my littleness. True, I was some five times smaller than him, though the King was twice as big as he was.

70

One day at dinner, he picked me up when no one was looking and dropped me into a large silver bowl of cream; then he ran off as fast as he could. If I had not been a good swimmer I could well have drowned; fortunately, Glumdalclitch saw my plight and fished me out after I had swallowed a few cupfuls of cream. The dwarf was soundly whipped and, as further punishment, forced to drink the bowl of cream.

Another hazard I had to face were the flies: the land was much pestered by flies in summer; these horrible insects, each as big as a sparrow, hardly gave me any peace at meals, constantly humming and buzzing about my ears. They would sometimes land upon my food and leave their disgusting eggs or mess behind, which I could see clearly even though the natives could not.

Sometimes they would land on my nose or forehead, leaving their slime by which they can walk feet upwards on a ceiling; the smell was horrible.

It was a favourite trick of the dwarf to catch some flies in his hand and let them out suddenly right under my nose so as to frighten me and amuse the Queen. My remedy was to cut them to pieces with my knife as they flew in the air; I became quite skilful at it.

I remember one morning, when Glumdalclitch had set my wooden house upon the window sill to give me air, that I was sitting at my table eating a slice of sweet cake when about twenty wasps came flying in through my window, attracted by the cake. Some seized large pieces of the cake and carried it away; others flew about my face trying to sting me.

At once I rose and drew my sword, attacking them in the air. I killed four of them before the rest escaped. Shutting my window after throwing out the dead bodies, which were as large as partridges, I then pulled out their stings from my skin and found them to be an inch and a half long and as sharp as needles.

The land of Brobdingnag

The kingdom of Brobdingnag is a peninsula bounded in the north east by a ridge of mountains some thirty miles high with volcanoes on the tops. On the three other sides it is washed by the ocean; the seas are generally so rough and full of jagged rocks that there is no venturing out to sea in ships. So the people are totally cut off from the rest of the world.

They seldom fish in the sea since the sea fish are the same size as those in England. But now and then they take a whale that is dashed upon the rocks. These whales are so large that a man can hardly carry one on his shoulders.

The country is well populated, for it contains fifty-one cities and a hundred walled towns. The capital, Lorbrulgrud, stands upon two equal parts each side of a river; it contains over eighty thousand houses and is some fifty-four miles long (or three *glonglungs* in their measure).

I was often taken by Glumdalclitch in a coach about the streets of the city. The worst sight was the beggars who would crowd round the coach as it passed. One woman had a pock-marked face whose holes were so big I could easily have crept into them. There was a fellow with wooden legs each about twenty feet high. The most awful sight was the lice crawling on their clothes: I could clearly see the legs of these creatures with my naked eye; their snouts were just like those of pigs rooting in the mud.

I should have been happy enough in that country if my size had not exposed me to several silly accidents. One day Glumdalclitch left me on a lawn while she walked at some distance with her governess. In the meantime a violent shower of hail suddenly fell; the hailstones gave me such cruel bangs all over my body that it was like being pelted with tennis balls. I was so bruised from head to foot that I could not go out for ten days.

A more dangerous accident occurred one day in the same garden. My little nurse again left me to enjoy my own thoughts and, while she was away, a small white spaniel belonging to the head gardener swept me up in his mouth. He ran straight to his master, wagging his tail and setting me gently on the ground. By good fortune he had been well taught and I was quite unharmed. This incident determined my nurse never to let me out of her sight again.

The maids of honour often invited Glumdalclitch to their apartments, begging her to bring me along too. They loved to see and touch me, even strip me naked from top to toe, as they would a doll. They seemed to have no shame in changing their clothes or bathing in front of me. I have to say it was a far from pretty sight. Their skins appeared so coarse and uneven, blotchy and hairy; a mole would be as broad as a ditch with hairs hanging from it thicker than horse hair – to say nothing of the rest of their bodies. And the smell from their skins was so unpleasant; mind you, their natural smell was far better than when they used perfume which made me faint at once.

It reminded me once again of Lilliput where a little friend once complained politely of the strong smell from me.

The greatest danger I met was from a pet monkey. I was sitting in my little house by the open window one day when I heard something bouncing up and down on the window sill. All at once, a great hairy face appeared at every window of my house, grinning and chattering. I quickly retreated into the far corner of the room, but the monkey – as big as an elephant – reached in and grabbed my coat lapel, dragging me out. I think he took me for his young by the way he stroked my face gently with his paw.

Startled by a noise, however, he leapt out of the window, clambered up the drainpipe and on to the roof; he settled down on the rooftop, holding me like a baby in one paw and feeding me with the other. He tried to cram into my mouth some vile mess he took from his own mouth; when I tried to spit it out he only crammed more in.

I heard a startled shriek from Glumdalclitch below as she caught sight of me on the roof. Soon several men were mounting ladders and the monkey, seeing himself surrounded, let me drop: I tumbled down the steep roof and landed in the guttering, some five hundred yards above the ground. At any moment I expected to be blown down by the wind. But a bold young footman climbed up and, putting me into his trouser pocket, brought me down safely.

Weak and bruised on all sides, and vomiting from the filthy stuff the monkey had forced down my throat, I had to take to my bed for a fortnight. It was only thanks to my dear nurse's care that I recovered.

The Queen, who often used to hear me talk of my voyages at sea, one day asked me whether I would like a boat of my own. I was delighted. So she had a carpenter make one, along with a wooden trough some three hundred feet long, fifty broad and eight deep. Henceforth I would often row for my own amusement, not to mention that of the Queen and her

75

ladies who would give my sail a fair breeze with their fans or even blow me across the lake.

The King, who enjoyed good music, often arranged concerts at court which I sometimes attended. But the noise was so great that I could barely make out the tunes. I am sure that all the drums and trumpets of the Guards could not equal it. In my youth I had learned to play the spinet and, since the palace had one, I thought I would entertain their majesties by playing an English tune. This was not so easy, for the keys were a foot wide and the keyboard sixty feet long. However, I made two clubs covered with a mouse's skin, and ran up and down a bench, striking the notes as I passed. The tune greatly pleased the King and Queen.

The King, who was a man of patient understanding, would often enquire about the affairs of my country. He would have my house brought into his room and put on a table so that I was level with his head. I would sit on a chair on the roof of my house and, in this way, we would hold long discussions about government, laws and education.

I began my story of England by informing him that we consisted of two islands. I told him of the English Parliament, partly made up of the House of Lords, persons of the noblest blood and oldest houses; the other part was an assembly called the House of Commons. These members were all important gentlemen, picked for their great abilities and love of their country to represent the whole nation.

The King took much interest in what I said; each of my five audiences with him lasted several hours, with the King taking notes of what I said. He wondered whether the lords I spoke of were promoted because of their knowledge of religion or whether they had been slaves to some nobleman whose opinions they continued to follow even after entering the Lords. He also asked whether gentlemen might not sacrifice the good of their country to the designs of a weak and vicious king.

On our laws he said that since all our judges were from the upper classes, did that not make one law for the rich and one for the poor? He wondered to hear me talk of such costly wars. Why was I so proud of them? We must be a quarrelsome people or else live among very bad neighbours. Above all, he was amazed to hear me talk of keeping an army in times of peace, and among a free people. He said that if we were governed by our own consent by people we had elected, he could not imagine against whom we were to fight. Would not a man's house be better defended by his own family than by half a dozen rascals picked at random from the streets?

He was perfectly astonished with the account I gave him of our affairs during the last century; he protested it was just one heap of conspiracies, rebellions, and murders – the very worst effects that greed, cruelty, hatred, and ambition could produce. At last, he took me into his hands, stroked me gently, and said the following, which I shall never forget.

'My little friend, Grildrig, you have given an admirable account of your country. And you have clearly proved that ignorance, idleness, and vice are the proper qualifications for governing it. Your laws are applied by people who are interested only in breaking and avoiding them. It does not appear that a man has to have any one virtue to obtain a high post in England, much less that men become nobles through virtue, priests promoted through their learning, soldiers for their valour, judges for their honesty, Members of Parliament for love of their country.

'As for yourself, you have travelled widely and, hopefully, you have escaped many vices of your country. But I conclude that Englishmen are the nastiest race of odious little vermin that Nature ever suffered to crawl upon the surface of the earth.'

To try to win back the King's favour and show him how clever we English really were, I one day said I could teach him how to make gunpowder so that he would win many wars. He would be able to destroy whole armies, sink ships with a thousand men in each, cut through hundreds of bodies, blow out men's brains, and also tear houses to pieces and lay cities to waste.

The King was horror-struck. He was amazed at how such an insect as I could have such inhuman ideas, to be so unmoved by such scenes of destruction. He would rather lose half his kingdom than learn such a secret which he commanded me never to mention again. He said that if a man could make two ears of corn, or two blades of grass, grow where only one grew before, he would do more good than he could ever do by winning a war.

My strange escape from Brobdingnag

I had always believed I would one day regain my freedom; but I could never have guessed how it would come about.

I have to admit I was treated with much kindness by the King and Queen and the entire Court. Everything was done to make me feel at home; the King even hoped that another ship might come ashore with a woman in it who could be my wife. He wished to continue my breed. But I did not fancy being a canary in a cage for people to stare at.

I longed to be among people with whom I could talk on even terms, to walk about the streets and fields without fear of being trodden on like a frog or hedgehog.

My freedom came sooner than I expected and in the strangest way.

I had now been two years in this land. As my third year started, I went with Glumdalclitch and the royal party to the south coast of the kingdom. As usual I was carried in my wooden travel box with a ring on top for a page to hold. When we reached the sea, my poor little nurse caught a cold and had to take to her bed. She was most upset when she had to let a page take me in my box down to see the ocean.

Once on the beach, I told the page to leave me for a while as I intended to take a nap. No doubt he scampered off to look for birds' eggs. I shut myself up in my little house to keep out the cold and climbed into my hammock; in no time at all I was fast asleep.

Suddenly I was awoken by a violent jolt: someone was pulling the ring on top of my box. I then felt the box being lifted high in the air and borne forward at great speed. The first jolt had knocked me out of my hammock, and now I was being flung from side to side.

Several times I shouted at the top of my voice, but to no avail. Out of the windows I could see nothing but clouds and sky; and I could hear noises overhead like wings flapping. Then it dawned on me: some eagle had no doubt got the ring in its beak. It obviously intended to dash me upon the rocks, like a crab or other shellfish, and pick my flesh out of the shell.

The eagle's keen sense of smell had evidently told it there was meat inside the house.

In a little while I noticed that the noise and fluttering of wings had increased, and my box was being tossed up and down like a kite on a windy day. I also heard a few bangs and squeals, as if birds were fighting. Then all at once I was falling straight down at such breakneck speed that I lost my breath and my stomach was in my mouth. My fall ended in a terrible splash, louder than the Niagara Falls.

For a few moments I was in complete darkness before my box bobbed up and I could see light from the tops of my windows.

I was in the sea!

I guessed that the eagle had been attacked by two or three others and had had to drop me into the ocean.

84

If I was in danger before, now I was in even greater trouble. At any moment I expected my box to be dashed to pieces against some rocks or overturned by a rising wave; if just one window broke I would be done for. The water was already coming in from little cracks, and I did my best to stop the leaks. Fortunately they were not too big.

Even if I did manage to survive the sea for a day or two I could only look forward to a miserable death of cold and hunger.

Some four hours must have passed. And then, to my alarm, I heard a grating noise along one side of my box, and I fancied that I was being pulled or towed along in the sea. For every now and then the box would give a jolt, which made the waves rise near the tops of my windows, pitching me into darkness.

I had no idea what was happening.

Mounting a chair and putting my mouth as near as I could to the air hole in the top of my box, I called for help in a loud voice, and in all the languages I knew. I then tied my handkerchief to a walking stick and thrust it through the hole, waving it in the air. If any ship were near, the sailors might realize there was some unhappy soul shut up in the box.

Nothing happened, save that I continued to be tugged along. After about an hour one side of the box struck against something hard. I thought it was a rock. Then I plainly heard a noise on the roof, like that of a cable grating as it passed through the ring. My box began to rise in the air. At that I began shouting until I was hoarse; in return I heard a loud cry repeated three times: it gave me such joy as is impossible to describe.

I now heard someone trampling overhead, and then came a voice calling loudly through the air hole:

'If there be anybody below, let him speak.'

It was an English voice.

I said I was an Englishman cast by misfortune into the most astonishing adventure that anyone had ever undergone. I begged them to save me from the dungeon I was in.

Shortly, a hole was made in the box, large enough to pull me out.

The sailors asked me a thousand questions, amazed at the sight of me and the little house. I was equally amazed at the sight of so many pygmies: for such I took them to be, after having for so long accustomed my eyes to the monsters I had left. The Captain, Mr Thomas Wilcocks, an honest Shropshire man, saw I was in no state to answer questions and had me taken down to his cabin to rest.

I slept several hours and awoke much refreshed. It was now about eight o'clock in the evening, and the Captain ordered supper. He entertained me with great kindness, explaining how I had been saved.

'About midday,' he said, 'I was looking through my spy-glass and spotted what looked like a chest or barrel some way off. I thought it might contain biscuits or liquor. So I sent a longboat out; my men returned, swearing they had seen a swimming house, with windows and a door. So we towed it to the ship.

'Imagine our astonishment when we saw the stick and white handkerchief thrust out of the roof. We imagined some unhappy soul had been cast adrift for his sins. Now tell me, Sir, what is your story?'

I begged his patience, and told him the whole tale from start to finish, from the last time I left England to the moment he first spotted me. Since he was an honest man he immediately believed my story. But, to convince him further, I had my wooden chest brought up from my box.

In his presence I opened it and showed him the little collection of rarities I had made in Brobdingnag.

There was the comb I had made out of stumps of the King's beard fixed into parings of her Majesty's thumbnail.

There was a collection of pins and needles from a foot to half a yard long.

Four wasp stings.

Some combings of the Queen's hair.

A gold ring which her Majesty had given me, taking it from her little finger and putting it over my head. I begged the Captain to accept the ring in return for his kindness.

A footman's tooth about a foot long and four inches in diameter.

Lastly I showed him the trousers I had on, which were made of a mouse's skin.

The Captain was well satisfied with my story and exhibits, and begged me to put down my tale on paper the moment I returned to England. I said I thought there were already too many travel books in the country. However, I thanked him for his kind words and said I would think about it.

One thing that struck him as odd was that I spoke so loudly: were the King and Queen of the country so hard of hearing? I explained how I had got used to talking as a man in the street would to another looking down from a church spire. For my part it seemed the Captain and his men were speaking in whispers.

It was full nine months since my rescue before we arrived back on the Downs of England: on the third day of June 1706. I took leave of the Captain and sailors, hired a horse and cart for five shillings and set off for home.

As I travelled along the road I marvelled at the tiny houses, the trees, the cattle, and the people. I began to think myself in Lilliput. I was even afraid of treading on every traveller I met, and I often called out to them to move out of my way lest I trod on them. I could well have received a few thick ears for my cheek.

When I came to my own house, I bent down to go in (like a goose under a gate) for fear of hitting my head. My wife ran out to embrace me, but I stooped lower than her knees, thinking she could otherwise be unable to reach my mouth.

I looked down upon the servants as if they were pygmies and I a giant.

It all goes to show how great is the power of habit. In a little while things gradually returned to normal. My poor wife begged me never to go to sea again; and though I promised to give it good thought, I knew my wandering nature would not keep me home. Indeed, there were more strange adventures lying ahead of me.

For the moment, though, my travels had come to an end.

Plate.I Part.I *Page.*I.

Hogs I

P Mintaon
I Good Fortune

I Naſſow
SUNDA
Sillabar

Straits of *Sunda*

Blefuſcu

Mendendo   Liſliput.

Diſcovered, A.D. 1699.

SUMATRA

Diemens Land.